I0730722

MONSTER FANTASTIC

BRADLEY DAVENPORT

ISBN: 978-0-9997967-8-8

for Mom & Dad

Also by Bradley Davenport

Brown Ridge: Shootin' Noise

Disclaimer

This is a work of fiction.
Resemblances to any peoples is purely coincidental

BRADLEY DAVENPORT

GROOVY TIME

1

"Trust me, babe, you'll love it!"

"It better be good, Ethan," Brandy laughed. "You're paying."

"Somehow I got pulled into that one. No, you're going to thank me later."

"Swear?"

"Promise."

"I'm gonna hold you to that."

"Hey, I'm never wrong about this stuff, babe."

Brandy and I were standing in line at Gold Plex AWC Emporium getting tickets to the re-release of *Night Crawlers*: A movie about blue monsters that stalk the night, looking for victims to take away to outer space. The movie was originally released in 1977 to a poor reception. Over the years, the movie became a cult classic. For the twentieth anniversary of the film, they brought it back to cinemas for one month only. There was an article I'd read that said they would be doing another sequel to the movie; there were already four of them. For me, I couldn't wait. I loved those movies. There was something magical about them.

We had our popcorn and soda in hand. I was never a fan of buying the candy. If I wanted to eat candy I would've bought some at the store and brought it. To be honest, I could've used a cheeseburger and a beer. I asked my girlfriend if she wanted to eat somewhere beforehand, but she wanted to wait until after. I didn't want to argue so I agreed.

I first discovered the movie late one night on cable when I was fifteen. After watching it, I had to go to the local video rental place so I could rent it. I had that video for over two months and had acquired a hefty late fee. *Night Crawlers* was considered a "must-see" for any movie buff.

We finally made it to the ticket booth, paid the money, and got the passes. We walked up to the ticket taker. He pointed and said our movie was the last door on the right. We walked down the long red hallway. We passed a big white framed poster that had two guys wearing overcoats and fedoras with their guns drawn toward one another. Under the two men in black lettering read: YOU CAN'T OUTRUN YOUR PAST. Behind the men was a shadow outline of a city. The title on top read: *Lonely Night.*

The frame beside the two gangsters was a black affair with a few fellas dressed in silver suits with laser guns, above them were three purple aliens looking with conscientious eyes. The title was *A Better Place.*

The frame on the wall directly across from space one, was a white canvas with a black silhouette of an overweight man with a hand on his head. On the other side of the canvas was a woman pointing her finger at the man. A word bubble hung over her head. The bubble didn't have any lettering. I guess they wanted you to fill in your own words. The title was at the top in red bubble font: *Tick O' Tat.*

Beside the door we were going to walk through was a black canvas with a big white house in the middle. A crazed man with a dark hat and a knife loomed over the top of the house. He had the knife pointed down at the house. Two spots on the house looked like slash marks. The face of a woman was in the bottom right corner. Her face looked like she was in the middle of a scream. In the middle, in blood letters, the title read: *Creep.*

We entered the auditorium walked down the red carpet to a middle aisle and sat. The lights and small beads of glass snaked themselves around the room. Dim light poured from the ceiling. We talked in low voices to each other through the ads, commercials, and movie trailers.

When the time came for the movie to start the beads of light lowered more, and the theater became dark. A bright white flash came on the big screen, starting the movie studio logos, and then, the production company. I looked at Brandy, and her eyes were fixed on the screen.

Two hours and fifteen minutes later the movie ended. We stood as the lights came up. As we walked out of the theater we talked about where we wanted to get a bite to eat. We went to this diner, Spring Rose, two blocks from where we were.

2

Orange rays broke through the morning sky as I stood outside of Bee Bee's, the gas station where I worked. As I finished my coffee and cigarette, I looked at the morning traffic passing by.

The business on the left side of Bee-Bee's was Manimal Eats & Games: A restaurant and arcade rolled into one. For the most part, the place was for kids, but, they had something for everyone. They served all sorts of foods— burgers, steak, pizza, chicken, fish, and a lot more. Prices were reasonable. The place had a few mascots: a cat, a bear, a rabbit, a dog, and a duck. The animals would put on a show for guests. They played instruments and sang. Employees of the place would dress in the costumes. Some friends of mine worked there over the years. They all liked it. Beside Manimal sat a small retail store called Jiz. On the other side of Bee Bee's was Steak Smack; besides that, another fast-food place, Cones. Across from Bee Bee's sat an auto shop; beside that, an insurance company, and then a bank. Further down the street was Stone Grill, an all-night restaurant. A strip mall followed; it housed various shops and eateries.

At the corner of Main and Elmer was the

high school, and then Eagles, a grocery store. When you drove up Elmer, over the hill, sat a few factories: One made shoes, one made computer parts, and another made jeans and t-shirts. On the other side of Jiz was a small pawn shop. Next to the pawn shop was a twenty-four-hour laundry mat, a motel, a butcher shop, and a post office. There was a big warehouse further down that was being converted into a theater. One of the movie houses on the other side of town was closing its doors.

The morning traffic got thicker as I stood smoking. A few cars and trucks had their windows rolled down with radios going. I looked at my watch and saw it was eight-thirty. I tossed my cigarette stub on the ground and walked toward the station.

The guy coming off the overnight shift, Quinn Poole, met me at the door. He was a slender fella, about 6'1, light brown hair, unshaven, and always looked relaxed. He wanted me to join him for a smoke. He gave me a run-down of how business was for the eight hours he was there.

"Hope it goes by fast for you," he told me.

"Me, too," I said. "I'm thinking it'll be like normal. It's how Mondays go. Craziness for awhile. Maybe a few drive-offs. Just another day..."

"Hell, that's every day around here. Had three people do that last night."

"Damn."

"Yeah."

"I had two the other day. People think gas grows on trees or some shit. The fuck people thinking?"

"It's a shame. Yeah, that shit doesn't cost money or anything. They need to set it up where you have to pay before you pump."

"That'd be the thing to have."

"See those fucks try to steal then."

"They'd probably find another way."

"Maybe."

"If they focused on doing good, this would be a better world."

"Got that right."

A black car pulled up to one of the pumps. The driver went inside.

"Who else is in there?" I looked at Bee Bee's.

Quinn looked at the building. "Josh is. Got here about five. He's about to leave, though. The dude said he had to go to his other job at noon."

"Where else does he work?"

"Not sure."

"I'll have to ask him."

"He doesn't talk to me about anything. I think he thinks I don't like him."

"Why do you think that?"

My friend looked down at the pavement. He started to study a rock before he kicked it across the parking lot. "I'm not sure. I always get this bad vibe. That cookout by the lake that time, I thought he wanted to fight. I didn't know what he was on. Hell, for all I know he just blasted a bunch of shit into his arm."

"That sounds about right. That's up his alley. But I'm not sure what day you're talking about."

"Think about it for a minute."

I looked at him, trying to remember the cookout he was talking about. But there had been a lot. I didn't know which one.

We laughed it off.

A car's horns started to honk. I turned around to see a line of cars motionless. Too many people trying to go in the same direction.

"They need more lanes," I looked back at my friend.

He looked at the street. "Won't ever happen. Can't get anything done here."

"Maybe if the city paid their people better," I said. "Something tells me that'll never happen. Can't pay people shit and expect hard work."

"That's what I was always told."

We talk a little more before he walked over to his car. He told me that we needed to get a burger sometime. I told him that sounded good. He got into his car and sped away into the morning.

3

I did a few menial tasks: made coffee, stocked newspapers, and stocked the milk and candy. The whole time I had to break from what I was doing to help check someone out.

At that time in the day, customers weren't talkative. After a few customers left I turned on the little radio behind the front counter. I tuned into WZZB, where Classic Rock lives! A friend of mine, Joey Ryder, hosted the morning show. He told me I should come by and advertise my movie on the airways when I was ready to promote it. I listened to my friend do his morning spiel about the morning and local events.

The week-long fair was in town. It was going to be fun for everyone, especially the little kiddos. They can throw darts, burst balloons, and get a cheesy stuffed animal. There were many booths and prizes. They could take their turn trying to hit the lever, launching the guy into a pool of water. Kids could take turns shooting a mounted shotgun, trying to sink a duck. Along with the games and rides, there was all the food. Your kid can get all the candy and fried treats they want.

Throughout the week there was a rodeo, a car show, and a derby. They had concerts

spread throughout the week. There were going to be clowns doing tricks and a dance
contest.

The last time I went to the fair, I woke up
the next day in jail. I was drunk and got into
a fight. As Joey gave off the list of musicians
for the concerts, I poured a cup of coffee. I
glanced out the big window as a shiny black
SUV pulled up to one of the gas pumps.
The man who crawled out of the vehicle had
short hair and dark sunglasses. It took me a
second to realize it was my friend, Doug
Wheetley. Doug and I had known each other
for about six years. We met in high school.
We were in the same graduating class.

When he finished pumping gas he came
through the sliding doors. He walked over to
the cooler, opened it, grabbed a few sodas,
and walked to the counter. He looked like
he'd been up all night partying. He was unshaven and looked tired. His eyes looked
fuzzy.

"How's it going?" I said.

"Not bad," he said. "The same thing every
day. I didn't die, so there's that."

"That's always a good thing."

"I need these," he said as he placed the
drinks on the counter.

"And two packs of smokes."

"What kind?" I turned to the rack of cigarettes.

"Let's do two of the Camels."

"You got it," I grabbed both packs, then turned around. "Just these and the sodas?"

"And the gas."

"Can't forget about that, can we?"

"You can always give it for free."

"Wish I could," I said. "They'd kick my ass outta this place."

He laughed. "I've heard stories about it."

"What?"

"I mean, some of the other people that had been fired from here."

"There's been a few, yeah."

"Sucks for them."

"They knew better. It doesn't take a genius to figure that one out."

"It'd surprise you."

"Maybe I should just steal the gas, smokes, and the junk food."

"Way to be a rebel!" Doug said. "We can learn a few things from you, boy. You got all this figured out."

"Think I'd be doing everyone a favor."

"Sounds about right."

"If they knew I did it, it would be anarchy. They'd have to close because there'd be nothing left to sell. I'd have to get a new job."

He asked if I had a part for him in movie I was filming. He told me how all the ladies would swoon when they saw him on the big screen. I told him I had the perfect part for him, that I wanted him to play a monster. He was beyond grateful. After I did some more work we sat around talking about the movie.

That night we shot a few of his scenes. He told me how much he loved it. He told me I needed to hurry up and complete the movie, so I could start my new carreer.

4

My friends and I thought we could rule the world. Nothing could stop us, or so we thought. The world was our candy store. We didn't know much about the future. We were young and wild. It was a great time to be alive. There was always something to be and somewhere to go. We were always try-ing to better ourselves. We were always looking for adventure. There were always people to hang out with. We would party at anyone's house or a local bar. People were always coming and going.

A few of us were hanging outside of Flipp's diner when our friend, Ryan, said we should get drunk on a bottle of whiskey he had in his car. About halfway through the bottle the cops came by. My friends and I freaked out. I knew we were busted. The people inside the diner must have called the cops. They pulled up, got out of their cars, and headed inside. We were shocked. They were getting a bite to eat. When everyone figured out what happened, we had a big laugh. We de-cided not to press our luck and left.

After we were away from the diner, back at Ryan's place, we discovered that he had two bricks of cocaine in the trunk of his car. We all started to give him the business about it, saying, "You could've gotten in big trouble for that," and. "They would've sent you to prison for a long time."

Ryan was telling us that they wouldn't put him away. The whole thing was a big joke to him.

We continued drinking and talking. I was at a three-day party with a bunch of friends. I knew it was getting out of control when they started to bring out the firearms and shooting into the air.

Some of the most dangerous mixers are booze and guns. No one called the cops, and it was good they didn't. The people I'd graduated high school with still lived in the area. Some had moved away, others in jail. I could tell you that the ones in jail were going to spend the rest of their lives in and out of various correctional facilities.

One night, I was out drinking with a few people at Mojo Fyv when two guys decided to race their cars.

The rest of us watched from the side of the street. As the two approached the finish line one of them flipped his car. He didn't die, but he spent the remaining years in a wheel-chair: it was a sad situation. The other guy in the race that night, Phil Dotts, felt terrible about what happened. He was out one night and got a thirty-year sentence for acciden-tally shooting a guy in the belly outside of a pool hall. Phil had always been a crazy guy.

We used to gamble a lot. We would always have a weekly game going at some-one's house. This one night, we were at Phil's when he turned a shotgun on us. Phil had gotten mad at our friend, Travis, who he claimed had cheated. When Phil pulled his gun, he made it clear there were a bunch of guns around the house and that if we moved or tried to leave, he'd shoot us all. After an hour, he let us go. I was still shocked when I walked out of the house. After that night, my friends and I distanced ourselves from Phil. A few weeks later, he was off to prison.

Another friend of mine, Josh Brinkley, went out with us drinking. After a night full of booze and weed he yelled out of my speeding car at a pair of girls walking down the street. "Hey, babies! You two are hot! Sexy!"

Both girls were thin with Blonde hair.

"Turn this around," Josh said. "We have to see what they have. Maybe they want to hang out, you know?"

I nodded. "You got it, buddy," I pulled a U-turn in the middle of the street and headed back.

"Hell yeah," our friend, Tyrone, turned up the radio. "Party all night, buddy! You gotta get it, get it, get it!"

We pulled alongside the girls and asked if they wanted to have some fun. They hopped in. We went to a few places and drank more.

A few nights later, I got a knock on my front door. When I opened the door, Josh was standing on the other side. I invited him in. He was nervous and sweating. I asked hiwhat was wrong. At first, he didn't say anything, then he took off his shirt and turned his back to me. Josh had four lash marks on his back. I asked what happened. After I made some coffee, he explained one of the girls we picked up that night, Ashley, and he went out two times. A few nights earlier, they were at her house having sex. The next thing Josh knew, some other guy came into the house. The guy turned out to be Ashley's husband. He caught the both of them. The husband took his belt off and started to slap Josh on the back. He was able to break free and get out of there. He went to the hospital. From what he said, he was bleeding and in a lot of pain.

There were a lot more crazy things that went on during that period. We were just a bunch of crazy people enjoying life, figuring out where we fit in the world.

5

It was 1997: I was twenty-two years old. I was going to be twenty-three in the summer. Brandy Kirby was going to be the same age. Her birthday was in October.

I was having the time of my life: not a care in the world. Brandy and I had been together for three years at that point. We had just moved in together. We rented a little two-bedroom at the end of Delaney Street. We used the spare room as an office/television room: Two couches, a big screen television, and a computer and desk made up the room. We always watched movies and things with friends. We would all get together, get some booze, and any other party favors anyone wanted to bring and make a night of it. We had a table to play cards in the corner of the room.

Along with many friends I always hung out with, acquaintances were always around. There were plenty of people to enjoy the nights with. We took turns; it'd always be at someone else's house every week.

My brother, Wayne, and I spent two weeks editing *Monster Fantastic*. The movie was about a group of monsters from space who crashed and landed in a forest on Earth. They couldn't repair their ship, so they lived in a shack. A few teenagers came to the forest to explore when they stumbled upon the monster's shack. The monsters capture the teens; and then the teens tried to escape. The plot wasn't complex. Even though it was a lot of work, I loved making the movie. My brother and I would spend the day drinking beer and editing the film in my office.

When it came to getting the editing machine, I had to get the cheapest I could find. One of the first things I decided was to do the flick in black & white to save money. Even though I was doing many things to save money, it still cost a lot. I wanted to break into the movie business in the worst way. I had a good imagination. Writing always came natural to me. I had a list of projects. But I had to get people interested in *Monster Fantastic* before I could move forward. Luckily for me, Bencroft had its own film festival. I just had to turn the movie over to Clyde Kemp. Clyde ran the festival. Since its conception in 1995, the festival was responsible for launching the careers of about twenty filmmakers. Clyde told me the nights when my movie would play. I told my friends and everyone I knew to attend.

The festival was called Bencroft Spectacular. The week my movie was showing, nearly thirty low-budget movies were going to be shown. The main theater where they showed the films was Bronson Hall: it sat three hundred people, and every seat was

full. Before the showing I gave a little intro-
duction.

After the movie I opened the room for some questions and answers. The bulk of the questions concerned my back story and filming. The whole thing was pretty neat. I was pretty proud of myself. They movie I'd made gained interest with people.

Clyde came on stage to give a final spiel about me, telling everyone he thought I had great talent.

I had a chat with Clyde after everyone was dismissed. He'd let me know when he had any luck selling my movie. After we left the festival, we went out drinking to celebrate. That was one of my best moments. I'd com-pleted my first movie and thought nothing could stop me. I felt like I could rule the world if I wanted.

6

Brandy and I pulled into the drive at Heather and Wayne's place. The house was a red brick two-story that rested at the end of a long, meandering street. The front lawn was free of trees, and most of the grass was dead— which made my brother happy because he didn't have to mow. Heather didn't care for the house. She always talked of wanting to move. The house wasn't in the best part of Bencroft. A little passed where they lived, on the next street, started what some referred to as "the hood" or "the slum." A lot of the houses in that area were used as drug dens and homeless motels. You could go over there anytime to get a fix of your pleasure: weed, cocaine, meth, acid, crack, heroin, whatever your vice was. Cheap hookers often populated the area. As soon as the cops shut someone down, another person would take their place. It was a mess.

As we pulled up to the house, I saw my friends had arrived. Their cars were parked in the dead grass and the driveway. We parked on the street in front of their place. We got out of my car and trampled up the drive. Two big bushes were on either side of the walkway that led to a small set of stone steps. Moths gathered around the small light that hung by the front door.

I gave three loud knocks. I wondered what craziness awaited me on the other side. The night before, Heather invited us to the Funhouse to see a friend of hers, Donalyn Massie, do some poetry readings. Donalyn had just moved from Texas to North Brown Ridge—about thirty minutes away from Bencroft. By what Heather said, Donalyn had a bad break with a boyfriend and needed to get away. Heather said we'd like her and that she was a great girl.

Muffled music came from the other side of the door. "Sounds like they started without us," Brandy said.

"Yeah," I smiled. "The fucking nerve of them."

She laughed. "Those assholes. What were they thinking?"

The door opened and my brother was on the other side, beer in hand. "How's it going, guys?"

"Pretty good," I said. "You?"

"The same," he replied.

"Seems to be the consensus around here." We shook hands.

He looked at Brandy. "Glad you could make it."

"Anytime," she said. "Always a joy, Wayne. Oh, yeah, I guess we had nothing better to do. I'm kidding. I need to keep my eyes on this one," she poked me in the stomach with her finger. "Have to make sure he doesn't get in trouble."

I turned to her. "Me? In trouble? I don't know what you're talking about. I'm a good boy. You don't have to worry about me, babe."

"Famous last words."

My brother moved from the doorway to let us in. "It's funny, I love it. I couldn't ask for anything more."

I shook my head. "I get it. This is where it's happening tonight,

right?" I passed through.

Brandy followed.

Wayne shut the door. "Welcome, welcome. Come one, come all! We've planned a de-lightful evening of entertainment! Prepare yourselves. It's

times like these that make it the best. I couldn't ask for more, good times with good people."

We agreed.

Wayne walked over to the fridge, opened it, got a couple of beer bottles and handed them to us. We talked some before we joined the others. We caught each other up on what went on that day. Wayne asked if I heard anything from Clyde yet. From whaat I knew he hadn't sold the movie yet. Some-thing told me that eventually it would hap-pen. I'd later learn that those things happen all the time. The wait is killer.

We stepped out of the kitchen and into the dining room. We
 passed a lonely desk piled high with papers and books. A red rug rested underneath the dining room table. A giant globe of light hovered over the room. The warm light filled us, crawling over every inch, digging into every crack and crevasse. The indoor plants sat potted on window ledges.
 When we walked into the living room Doug jumped from the chair he had been sitting in, telling us it was about time we got there.
 "I know," I told him. "Sorry about that."
 "I was beginning to think you guys were going to be a no-show. I asked Wayne about it a few times. I was going to have to send out the cops, start a search mission, or some shit."
 "We're here now," my girlfriend took my hand. "Your
 friends are safe."
 "It wouldn't have been the same without you. I won't be forced to spend the night alone with these losers. You guys can join the fun. We're getting a little twisted before we head out."
 "I see that," I looked at the beer in his hand.
 "That's the way we do it. We go all the way," he went on to tell us.
 "A little?" Heather stood from the couch.

"Looks like you've had your fill. You need to slow down, sir. I don't want you to pass out before midnight. You'll be puking all over here. I'm not cleaning up after you."

"Yes, I've had my share but can't slow down, not when we have a full night of activities ahead, you dig? I'm the motherfucking champ of the world!" She looked at him and shook her head. "Just saying you might be overdoing it."

"Oh, honey, don't worry about me. I have complete control."

"That's fine, I won't bother you about it anymore. Don't say I didn't warn you."

"You better." He gulped some beer. "No problem here. Listen, I'll take what you said under consideration. I'm not going to promise anything. I got my shit under control," he pointed at Brandy and myself. "You guys, don't mind that mess Heather's talking. She just thinks the drink makes me crazy. If she'd ask anyone they'd tell her I don't need this stuff to get crazy. She needs to know what the fuck is going on. She's the crazy drunk around these parts. I'm one fine motherfucker!"

"Whatever you say, man," Heather shook her head. "Who was it that got black-out drunk the other night that I had to take care of?"

Doug said, "You guys say that was me... I don't know. I was

passed out by what you guys said. Can't be responsible for my actions."

"The man has a point," Quinn added.

Doug clapped his hands. "See, that's a smart guy."

"A wise man," Quinn patted Doug on the shoulder.

"Thanks for that," Doug said. "What are friends for?"

Doug was drunk.

Everyone laughed. They were both drunk.

The two ther people in the group that night were Sandy and Rory.

Rory was an ex-stripper. She had danced at a place called Purple Vine for five years. Rocky Thomas, the owner of Purple Vine used to mistreat the girls who worked for him. He didn't rape anyone, but he would constantly harass the girls in every manner. One night, Rory slapped him in the face and walked out. The next day Doug asked me to go with him to visit Rocky at his house. The conversation got heated, and Rocky pulled a gun. Before he could Doug hit him to the ground. We walked out and left his front door open. Three months later, one of the girls who worked for Rocky filed charges against him. He got five years for assault.

Sandy, on the other hand, was a different story. She had grown up in Bencroft and spent her whole life there. She was in my graduating class in high school. In school, I

had a bit of a crush
 on her. She was a cheerleader. She had a
thin frame and long legs. Her long red hair
and pale skin looked great. She always
wanted to be a nurse. At one time, she was
going to school for it while working full-time
serving drinks at Gravity. She only had
about a year of school left when she
dropped out. I asked her once if she wanted
to be a doctor.
 She said, "Hell no! Too much school for
me. Why would I
 want to do that? Am I crazy or something?"
 As we continued to drink we told stories.
At one point, Doug told us that we needed
to blow-off the poetry thing and get on a
plane to Las Vegas.
 Rory looked at him. "Vegas, what are we
going to do there? You have the money to
buy all of us a plane ticket?"
 He told her he didn't, but it'd be cool if he
could. He told us we'd have the time of our
lives.
 A little while later Wayne told us it was
time to leave.

7

Ten minutes after we left my brother's, we pulled into the parking lot of the Funhouse. We staggered out of our cars into the fresh night. All sorts of characters were hanging around. There were people our age huddled in circles throughout the parking lot. They were standing outside vehicles, talking, laughing, and playing music. A few vagrants were standing at the side of the building, begging for money. Most people ignored them. A few felt pity and gave some loose change.

Cars and trucks were screaming down the highway beside us. A few people were sitting cross-legged in the lot reading poetry. Marijuana flowed from a parked blue car. One of the guys sitting in the circle talked about how a novel he wrote was published a few days earlier. He was sitting with a beer in hand, bragging to a couple of girls about the significant advance he received. A few people danced beside their car. One of them muttered something about having sheets of acid and what a beautiful night it was to be alive and swaying with the air. He kept rattling about how music is a passage-way to the enlightened mind. I thought about getting some of the acid, but decided it would be best not to.

The Funhouse was a large warehouse

that had been converted into a suitable business. We walked up the ramp to the double doors. A line started to form behind us. A guy was right outside the door checking IDs. After things were checked he let us in. When we got in, two other guys patted us down, checking to make sure we didn't have drugs or weapons.

The red walls inside the entrance had pictures, all faces of past performers. I scanned the photographs and saw some people I knew. I nudged my girlfriend to show her.

"Don't act like a tourist," she said.

"Sorry, babe."

"Dork!"

"That wasn't nice."

"You'll live."

"Sure about that?"

"Pretty sure."

"I just thought it was cool. I mean, I know some of these people."

"Maybe we could ask them for some money."

"It's worth a try," I told her.

She held my hand as we continued to walk.

The carpet was dark red, and lights hung from the ceiling. A full bar was on either side of the stage in front. Waiters and waitresses darted around, taking orders and getting food, coffee, and liquor. As we shuffled through the madness I spotted a table in front of the stage. I asked everyone if it would be a suitable place to watch the entertainment. We sat around the table.

After a few minutes a blonde waitress came by the table to take our order. She wore a tan blouse and a white miniskirt. "How are you guys tonight? My name's Sonja. I'll be taking care of you guys," she said, taking a pen and pad from her shirt pocket. "What can I start you guys out with? All of our beer is fifty percent off tonight."

"That's assuring," Doug said. "I like women taking care of me."

"Well, then, glad to help," Sonja said.

"I know that's right, man!" Quinn laughed.

Rory gave an annoyed look to her boyfriend. "Can you stop?"

"Stop what?" Doug said. "I'm just enjoying myself."

"Could you please not do all of that?" Rory sighed.

Quinn hit Doug on the arm. "You'll have to pardon my friend here, Sonja. He doesn't know how to act in public."

"Fuck you," Doug hit him back.

Sonja smiled. "It's okay."

I told her we'd just get a few pitchers of beer.

Sandy and Rory told their men not to act like fools. Our waitress said that sounded good. Before she left the table she told us if we needed anything else to let her know.

We scanned the place and saw some people we knew. We talked and laughed. It was a good time. When Sonja came back to the table Doug told her she needed to join us when she got off work.

People were sitting at the bar talking while waving their hands in the air. Another bartender came behind the bar and started making drinks. Two guys came on stage with guitars. They told us they'd play until the show began. They called themselves Winos of Time. They had a small following with some local places. I'd seen them at a few places before. The guys played four songs.

A man with light brown hair and Khaki pants walked on stage. "Is this thing on?" he asked into the microphone. "Testing, testing, testing for life out there. One, two, three, am I coming through okay? Can everyone hear me? We've been having trouble with the sound equipment. Just wanted to make sure everything is in order."

A guy from the back shouted. "It's fine! Get on with the show, fucktard!"

The man on the stage cleared his throat. "Before I get to the performers tonight, I just want to take time to thank all those good people who've helped keep this place alive by way of all the generous donations. Without you, let's face it, ladies and gents, this place would've been gone long ago. I can't express what this place means to me. This whole thing was thought up by me and a few others years ago."

Another patron shouted. "If you don't shut up, I'll be glad to donate my foot up your ass!"

The man laughed. "I think it's time to start. I don't feel like getting beat. If I do, everyone heard that guy say that. Yeah, I think it would be best if we started. Let me say again that we thank you very much. I'm sure all of you will enjoy yourselves. I'd also like to add this: It's important that we have things in life that inspire us. We need creative people in the world. Art, no matter the form, is essential. After we're all gone, art will still be here," he said, looking around the crowd. "Never give up on your dreams. I can't express that enough. The first guy to take the stage is a native of Bencroft. His name is Jimmy Davis. He's going to be doing two pieces, two original pieces. He's my cousin."

Jimmy took the stage and read two short poems. They were okay, I guess. Quinn and Doug weren't fans. Those two, they were making fun of Jimmy the whole time he was on stage.

A few other people came and went from the stage. They were all pretty good. They did their best. Actually, as I was listening to them I thought that I should get up there sometime and do some stuff.

Donalyn finally took the stage. She was in a black mini skirt and black blouse. A thin necklace and a small stud on the side of her nose were thrown into the mix. She had Navy blue eyes and red hair—which I found out was a dye job. Her natural hair color was brown. I liked the way her clothing wrapped around her thin frame.

 She smiled. "Hope everyone's doing great tonight. I want to begin by saying how excited I am to be here. It takes a lot of courage to get up here, to expose yourself, to be naked with your thoughts. I want to start by giving thanks to the people who run the Funhouse. Those guys do a lot of good for the community. I just recently moved here from Texas. This state has shown me a lot of love. I'm very grateful for this opportunity. When I first saw a flyer about this place it intrigued me. I decided to take a gamble. I hope it works out. I might be back to showcase more. The first of my works, it's something I wrote the other day called 'Windows.' I hope you guys like it."

The poem was five stanzas long. Her other poem was called "Sandwich." She explained the meaning was different for everyone listening. She explained how she had a series of numbered poems with this name. The poem was a retrospect of a year in her life. After reciting her poem she put the microphone on the stand and walked off.

A few guys from across the room whistled as she approached our table. By then, a few people had already spat out of the building, hurling themselves into the night, searching for things they could never get their hands on.

When Donalyn sat at the table everyone told her how much they loved the poems. She smiled and thanked us, saying that we just said that to be polite.

"No," I told her. "They were really good."

"Thanks."

We went around the table introducing ourselves. We ordered food and more drinks. We sat there until the place closed getting to know our new friend. I thought she was very beautiful. It's not eeryday that beauty like that walks into your life.

After we left the place we went back to Wayne's house where we drank more. We all got pretty fucked up.

8

I got a call from Clyde Kemp. He told me to come to his office for a talk about *Monster Fantastic*. I headed down to the office. It only took me twety minutes to get there. I was excited and nervous all at once. I wasn't what he was going to tell me, but something told me it was going to be good.

We greeted each other when I stepped into his office. He offered me something to drink. I told him coffee would be nice. He told hissecartary to make some coffee.

"Well, Ethan, I've been making calls all over about your movie. And I got a call back. A few friends of mine out in Califonia. They'd already seen your moviie and want to do business."

"Is that so?"

"It looks good," he told me. They want to meet with you as soon as you cam."

I nodded. "I can always take a break from Arkansas."

"I'll give them a call and let them know you're interest. When would be the earliest you could meet with them?"

"All the way over there? Oh, I'm not sure. I'd have to let Brandy know. But I'm thinking in about a week or so."

"okay."

We drank coffee and talked for a long time. He gave me the names of the people and wished me luck.

9

A few days later, Brandy and I got on a plane headed to California. I hadn't flown much and she hadn't either. We landed, checked into a motel, and then explored the town. We ended up at this little bar called Factory Wicked. We had a great time. Everything was bright and beautiful.

The next day we caught a cab and started toward where the meeting was. The driver was this odd-looking guy named Chuck. For some reason he needed to tell us everything about himself. I didn't want to be rude, so I played along.

"Guys, enjoying your time in town?" the driver said.

"It's been pretty nice," I told him.

"Guys new to the area?"

"We're just in town for a few days."

"Ah, I gotcha! You guys going to see some sights and stuff?"

"Maybe," I said.

He seemed interested. I told him about the meeting, and told him about the movie.

"Man, that's pretty cool," he said. "I've driven a lot of those famous people. Do you have big dreams of fame?"

I told him I wasn't sure, and that I'd just have to see how things went.

He went on to ask Brandy a bunch of questions about us. I thought it was a little strange, but figured he was bored and wanted someone to talk to. Being stuck in a cab all day must have its down side.

We talked more as we rolled down the street. Everyone who was out seemed to be enjoying themselves. Fast cars with tops down screamed music. Chuck went on to tell us about some of the more friendly clubs and bars in the area.

We pulled in front of a huge building that had sixteen or so floors.

"We're here," Chuck told us.

As we got out he wished us luck. He told us if we needed another ride to give him a call.

We walked inside. The desk lady took my name and said it'd be a minute. After about twenty minutes, a woman came out of an office and called my name. Brandy and I stood and followed her. We saw two guys sitting around a desk. They stood and introduced themselves. Brandy asked if it was okay if she stayed. They told her she was okay. The two men were Charles Mann and Sammy Hyde. We found out the girl's name was Cindy Weaver. Cindy was a portly black-haired woman who put on too much makeup. She said how she wanted to stay but couldn't. I guess she had better things to do.

"To begin with," Sammy said, "we'd like to thank you for making the trip. We know you're over in Arkansas. Was it a good trip?"

"It was fine," I said. "Thanks for the invite."

"Our pleasure," Sammy said with a smile. "We're glad you were able to enjoy our fine state."

"Oh, it's been good," my girlfriend said.

Sammy said, "It's a lot different from your home. I've never been to Arkansas but heard it's pretty nice."

"It's not bad," I said. "The weather's a pain at times. But you take the good with the bad."

"I hear you on that. We have our times here. But I've been here all my life. Don't think I'll ever move."

"Nothing wrong with that. Gotta stick to what you know sometimes."

"That's about it."

Charles said, "I moved from New York sixteen years ago."

"Why?" my girlfriend asked.

"Had this dream of getting into acting. Nobody would hire me. A few months later I fell into this gig. Well, not this job, exactly. I started in the mail room. I worked my way up."

"Looks like it worked out."

"It did. I wouldn't change anything now. Make good money. I'm still in the movie business. Sometimes I still think about how it would've been to be an actor."

"Let's get this show rolling, eh?" Sammy said, "A lot of thought goes into something like this, to make a business deal like this."

I nodded. "Of course."

Sammy continued. "We deal in the creative side

of things and the money involved. We tend to look at beginners closer than others."

"Understood," I said.

Charles interjected. "At the same time we love new blood."

"Thanks," I said.

"When Clyde first contacted us, I gotta say, we were very interested. He talked about it like it was his creation. We told him to send a copy over and we'd be glad to look at it."

Both of them said how much they loved the movie. They explained that they take low-buget movies and make them better through editing. After they showed the movie to their bosses they were told to meet with me. They passed me a contract for a three movie deal.

"We want you to be a part of the family," Sammy told me.

I read it and signed. I guess in retrospect I should've had a lawyer look it over. But I didn't really care at the time. I just wanted to get paid for what I loved doing.

We spent the next two hours bullshiting about movies and music we liked. They invited Brandy and I to lunch. After we ate Sammy told us about a party he was having at his house, and that we should attend.

"I can send a car over to your hotel," he told us.

Sammy lived in a massive house in Los Angeles. Many people were at the party, all coming and going, dancing and laughing while getting drunk out of their minds. Our host took us around, introducing us to movie business peo-ple: actors, writers, directors, and singers. We talked to whoever was around. As Brandy and I were making our way through the maze, people kept giving us booze.

At one point during the evening some girls started dancing to loud music, taking off their clothes, throwing themselves around the place. Everyone was getting wild. As the party was dy-ing down I asked Sammy if we could stay the night. He told us to take one of the rooms up-stairs. We found a bedroom, shut the door, and fell on the bed. We had wild sex until the sun came up.

We had lunch with our host and some other people when we woke. We went back to our ho-tel, and a few hours later we caught a cab back to the airport.

10

Over the next two months, I made four trips to Cali. I had fun while finishing *Monster Fantastic*. Five months after I sold my movie, I was watching it on opening night. Brandy and I snuck into the back of the theater and looked at the reactions. Everything went great. I was very pleased.

"I'm proud of you," she told me.

"Thanks, babe."

"It's inspiring."

"Not sure about that."

"No, you saw something you wanted to do, and you just did it. Even though it puts you in debt. You didn't know it was going to become anything. You took a chance."

"It was just something I wanted to do. No big deal."

"Still..."

"It was what I wanted to get myself into."

We sat through the closing credits as they rolled up the screen.

"It never dawned on me to sit through all of those names before. I mean, I'd always watched the first few names, sure. I can understand why they do now. We know those people. The next one will star me, right?" she giggled.

"You bet, babe," I smiled. "You'll win all the awards."

She brushed her hair from her face. "I missed

my calling. I should've studied acting in school.
I could be a millionaire. My name in bright
lights... A movie on the marquee. It'd be a glori-
ous thing."

"They offer classes at UB."

"Really?"

"Joey took it for a year."

"He likes it?"

"Yeah."

"It shows," she nodded toward the movie
screen.

"The guy knows what he's doing. You have to
give it to him. He was pretty convincing."

"Think he was the only one who read the whole
script. Think the others were just focused on getting famous."

"Hate to disappoint them, but..."

"Oh, I know."

"Should've told them not to hold their breath."

"Ummm, I dunno," I muttered.

"It could be the biggest movie in the world in a
week or two."

"Indeed."

"Awe, honey, how nice."

I placed my hand on hers. "That'd be incredi-
ble. I love the positivity. It's not going to happen. I can see it more when I have a few out
there."

The lights came up.

We stood and walked out.

"I think you were good in that one," I put my
arm around her.

"Well, thanks."

"Hey, all the thanks go to you. It wouldn't have been the same."

"That's sweet of you to say."

"Without you, it would've fallen apart. Yeah, the part was important. And the fact that my girlfriend played it made things a lot less stressful."

"Glad I could be of service."

"It helps to work with people you get along with."

"Couldn't agree more."

We got into my car.

"Where to now?" I turned to her.

"Wherever."

I placed my hands on the wheel. "Wanna get a bit to eat?"

"I can do that."

"Good deal.

We ended up going to a diner in Janson. We talked the night away while we drank coffee and ate pie.

By the next week, I was talking about my next movie in Sammy's office. My next feature was a script I wrote called *Night Sing*: It was about an alien invasion. The movie was about aliens who came to Earth from their planet light years away. When they reach our planet, they're met with a group of yellow monsters who want to rage into war. The yellow monsters don't want to share any spoils of the land they found. They assured all the people of Earth that if they did everything that was asked of them, they wouldn't die. A war starts between the aliens and monsters, with humans in the middle.

Sammy said, "It sounds good to me. Things like that always interested me. I like it. You don't even have to see a script. I'm sold. You got my money. That'll fill seats, buddy. How much were you thinking for a budget?"

"Guess I didn't think about that part," I said. "I don't really wanna spend much money. If I had to guess, I'd say the movie might lose money. I'd feel bad if you guys didn't get your investment back."

"How nice of you. Isn't it every day I hear that? I wish some others had the same manners."

"Not everyone's like me."

Sammy sat behind his desk. "Were you thinking of doing it big? Do you want a lot of effects and things?"

"There's going to be a few. I want to try it with as little as possible. I know those can get pretty costly."

"True," Sammy said. "But if it serves the movie. As you go further in this business, you'll realize that studios will shell out crazy money into their movies. Anything to make the product the best it can be."

"Makes sense," I said. "You'd wanna maximize, sure."

"All I ask is that you try not to exceed the budget."

"Oh, I won't."

"Happens more than you know. They always

say they won't, but they always do. They habitu-
ally do that, and pretty soon, no one wants to
work for them."

"Like I said, that won't be me. I want a good
working relationship."

"That's all I can ask for," Sammy said. "Been in
this business a long time, seen it all. Guys you
think will go on to be great, don't. Some do.
Lately, it's a rare thing. I want you to know what
you're getting pulled into. You know, it depends
on how far you want to go. You wanna try to
make a quick buck then be out, or you in this for
the long haul?"

"I wanna go all the way to the top. Why get into
something if you don't want to do your best at
it? I mean, if it's just about money, I could go
out and get any job I wanted. I want this, sir.
This is what I have the most passion for."

"We all have our corks.

We talked for a bit longer about how much
money to spend. We got to the point in the conversation where the question of casting came up.
I shook my head and told him I didn't know. He
said he'd set some stuff up and make some calls.

"Honestly, I hadn't even thought about that.
The first one, I just put people I knew in it."

"Don't worry," he said. "We have people who
do this all the time. We'll get a bunch of pictures
of actors and actresses. We bring them in to au-
dition."

"How long is that?"

He sat back in his chair. "It varies. It's all about

getting the best person for the part. I've seen it take less than two weeks, others a few months. I think, in this case, it won't take long," he looked at his copy of my script on his desk and put his finger on it. "Have any ideas of what you want in the cast?"

"Like I said, I dunno, hadn't given it much thought. When I had it playing, I thought the monsters should be tall."

"That right?"

I shook my head.

"A lot of makeup?" he asked.

"I guess. I wanted the monsters to have like a reptile look. Well, maybe not all of them. The others, just ugly green guys."

"That'll look good, sure. Anything to scare the kiddos. That's what sells the tickets. I always have to keep them comin' for more. That's how you get rich, buddy boy."

"A little more money would be nice," I told him.

"Well, you must remember that's not the most important thing. Yes, it's the thing that funds. Don't wanna be somewhere flippin' burgers, do yeah?"

"No."

"Of course not."

"If I did that, I wouldn't have time to create."

"It's the reality of it."

I let out a smile. "I got fired from the fast food job I had."

"Why'd you get fired?"

"I wasn't fast enough."

"Ha. That's key in that business."

I propped my right leg on my left knee.

"They'll get by without me."

"They call you back?"

"No."

"They'll be fine."

"Guess they will," I said. "I still have a job at this gas station where I live."

"You like it?"

I nodded. "I like it."

"You wanna keep it?"

"I'll just see how it goes."

"You have something good here. You can make things great for yourself."

"I know."

"A lot of money in this."

"I just wanna get my hands on some of it. I mean, don't get me wrong or anything; that's not the only reason I've taken this path. I love telling stories."

"Don't we all?"

We talked some more.

The whole process differed significantly from my first movie, mainly due to the studio's involvement. But the studio fronted the money, so I put up with their bullshit. I tried to get some of my friends in the movie, but the studio wouldn't have it. I wasn't that happy with any of it. The filming of *Night Sing* took about two months. After the production, the movie went into another three months of post-production. They asked if I wanted someone else to edit the film. I told them I wanted to do it myself. The way I figured it, I wanted to have total control over my art. I couldn't understand why anyone would hire someone to edit a movie they knew nothing about. People seemed to like what I did.

Within the first couple of months, it made its budget back—twenty-five million. It made a lot more money than my first one did. *Monster Fantastic* had only made a total of two million, but the thing made a huge impact on DVD sales. People came up to me on the street and told me how they liked both of my movies.

11

Over the next year, I divided my time between Arkansas and California. I didn't fit into California. No one there seemed to want anything to do with me. I felt normal in Bancroft, my home. Yes, a few fellow filmmakers respected me, but people didn't like what I was doing. I guess they didn't want my brand of blood. I would be invited to big lavish parties with directors and actors. We would drink wine and liquor and talk the night away about films and how we wanted to change the face of movies. This guy, Simon Wittenburg, an aging director, used to speak to me about the fruits of the business. He would tell me that if I didn't watch myself, I'd crash and burn.

I indulged a little, but I stayed to myself for the most part. He would have screenings at his house all the time. At all the screenings, about forty to fifty people would attend. We would have lengthy discussions about the film. When I left Simon's big house in the hills, I took long drives to clear my head.

I rented a small apartment at SunLand in Janson, California. Brandy stayed with me until she decided to return to our home in Arkansas.

We hated being apart, but we knew it had to happen at the time. We talked about her moving with me permanently, but she didn't want any part of it. We had a few heated arguments about the subject. One night, she got so mad she threw a glass against the wall and stormed out. She wanted to stay in the place she called home.

I couldn't say I could blame her. Everyone wants to be in a place they feel comfortable with. She said something that hurt my feelings; she said she wouldn't commit to a move based on the promise that my movie career would last. Anyway, we fought. I was mad. A few hours later, she was back on a flight to Arkansas. For a few weeks, she wouldn't return my calls. She finally called and told me that I better make this work. We talked for awhile, and everything seemed to be okay again.

When I first moved to California after selling my first movie, everyone told me I needed to get an agent. I ended up going with a guy named Allen Cocks. I came down to his office, and we had a discussion.

The one thing he had for me was the *Run, Run, My Man* television show. The show wasn't great at all. But I figured I had to pay my dues. I wasn't a fan of sitcoms; it was something that paid my bills, though. I had to get used to working with other writers. The show-runners hired a staff of twenty writers. We'd spend afternoons after lunch discussing comedic scenarios we could throw the characters into. I didn't get sole credit for writing any of the scripts. I found it hard to write comedy. The show only lasted one season before it was canceled. I guess the rest of America didn't like it. I can't say that, as I could blame them. The show was garbage. And it wasn't something I wanted to do in the first place.

One day, David Kay, a big-time filmmaker, came to my door in California. He said he heard I was renting an apartment and wanted to swing by. It turned out he wanted to take me out for lunch. He told me he'd be paying. I never shy away from a free meal, so I agreed. David was an older man, about fifty or so. He was a short man with a big white beard and glasses. He wore all black. We went to a fancy outside restaurant, Ol' Spoons. David went on to tell me that all the big famous people ate there. He said that he'd had lots of business meetings at the place.

When you first walk up the sidewalk, you'll see Spoons, with tables scattered all over its concrete slab. A few areas had giant umbrellas to block out the bright sun. A man sat behind a piano in the center of the place, playing soft sounds. A host greeted us at the entrance. The man ushered us to a table underneath one of the umbrellas. Both of us ordered tea. We had a nice lunch. After lunch, we returned to his big house and watched some movies.

12

Before I knew it, three years had passed. I had four movies under my belt by then. My other two movies, *Knock the Night* and *Into After*, didn't do well upon their release. The DVDs did pretty well through. I got a call to come to Sammy's office. I'd be lying if I said I wasn't nervous. I didn't know what to expect. I knew the fact that he wanted me to come to his office meant it was big. He could've just told me over the phone. I thought it might be some more work. Another movie? Maybe they wanted to give me some awards? Movie of the year? Hell, if I ever got that, I'd be shocked. In the business, I would make what's referred to as "B movies." Mostly, people weren't knocking down my door to work with me. I didn't want Sammy to offer me another series. I wouldn't say I liked that process. I remember when my agent first brought the series up to me; I told him I'd do it once but not after that; that's not why I got into the business.

I got to the building that housed Sammy's office. The place, like every time I'd been there, was busy. Loud chatter came from people walking through the lobby—all sorts of people, side-by-side, chattering into their cell phones. The phone at the front desk kept ringing. I walked to the desk and gave my name and what I was doing there. It had been a different girl working the desk I'd been there. That day, there was a red-head behind the desk. She was bubbly with thick lipstick. After some talk, she told me she had seen all my movies. She said she liked them. I thanked her and gave her an autograph.

She had me take a seat and wait.

About twenty minutes later, the redhead told me I could go back to Sammy's office.

We greeted one another. He looked as if he hadn't slept. He told me he'd been up trying to save a movie. I didn't ask which one.

"We need to talk," he told me.

"Is it that bad?"

"I think so."

"Oh, man. Okay, just hit me with it."

He explained to me that because the last two movies didn't do well in theaters, they decided to release the rest of the movies I made on video and DVD.

Sammy said, "I know it went well initially, Ethan, but it slowed down. I'm sorry. You know we've lost a lot of money from a dozen films in the last three years. Suits bigger than me were asking questions."

"Like what?" I asked.

Sammy sighed as he sat back in his chair. "Like whether or not these movies are that good. They see the losses and wonder if it's worth it in the long run. We're not singling you out or anything. We're talking to some of the other guys. From now on, all of your movies will be made straight into DVD and video formats. Like I was saying, those pull in some pretty impressive figures."

"But one of the reasons I got into this was to get my movies to play in theaters."

"I understand."

"Do you?"

"I do."

"You sure? You're saying the words, but I'm not sure you know."

"Believe me, Ethan, I wish it was better. But on the good side, we can still do business together."

We talked awhile longer before I left.

13

I decided I needed a long break. I went back to Bancroft. I'd just been so tired of everything about movie-making. I missed my home and friends. I needed to decide if I wanted to return or not. Brandy and I discussed it a few times. She would tell me she wanted me to do something that'd make me happy. After heavy debate, I decided not to continue making movies. I thought about what Sammy told me about making movies for the Web. I didn't want to do any of that. I decided to write my movies as novels. The idea I had, I could make the movie. I could be in charge of everything and not have to make compromises: Sound, lighting, characters, dialogue, setting, movement of people, and editing would be under my control. The budget could be as big or as small as I wanted. The writing factor I'd already done in the movie scripts, but now, I'd be able to do every piece of the scenery.

We went to a night spot called Wire. It was my usual small group of friends. It was going to be a great night. We were partly celebrating Joey's new job. He got another radio gig: WGNA in North Brown Ridge. I knew he could never quit radio altogether. I guess a little time away was all he needed. He enjoyed the new job. They had him for the graveyard shift. Joey had always wanted to do the radio overnight. It was a talk/rock n' roll show. We could all tell he was pretty pumped about it. He was nothing but smiles as he was telling us all about it. He told us he was a night owl and the best person for the job.

The Wire was a good place for dancing and loud music. The bar served a whole galaxy of booze, anything you could think of. The place had three bars: Two in the back portion of the building where the main dance floor was, and then one as you entered the place. You can find all sorts of characters on Wire. There was a great spirit about the place. When there wasn't a DJ spinning loud music, a band was playing. On the night we were there, a Friday, there were both The DJ in the back and the local band when you first walked in. Both parts of the bar had pool tables and a few dart boards.

As we were standing around the bar talking, out of the corner of my eye, I saw Donalyn approach us with other girls. They stopped, and we talked for awhile. Donalyn looked great—she always did. I thought her lips would taste great when you kissed them. I wanted to find out.

Donalyn held up her beer. "Cheers to you guys! What a fabulous night to see friends, right?"

Amy nodded. "It is that. What are you guys up to?"

"Getting our fill," the redhead said. "Why else would we be here?"

The other girls at Donalyn's party were two blondes and a pink-haired girl.

"We wanted to check out the outfit," one of the

blonde girls said.

"And to dance," the pink girl said. "I'd been wanting to come all week. I love to dance."

"Who doesn't?" Amy said.

Pink threw up her hands. "Yeah, we're gonna shake that nasty thing!"

"What she said," Amy smiled.

We made some small talk with the group.

We had lots of fun, lots of drinking and dancing. The girls in our group decided they wanted to shoot a few pool games. The guys, we sat at the table drinking, looking at the girls. We thought it'd be a great idea to gamble at darts.

"Okay, guys," Joey said. "Let the games begin. Wanna throw ten bucks in, see how it goes?"

I brought out a ten from my pocket. "Here's mine. I know he'd like some friends."

"You sneak that from the station?" Quinn looked at my bill.

"Shit," I said. "I don't need that guy's money. I have my own. You forget I've made a few flicks in my day."

Quinn laughed. "When you make a good one, I'll check it out."

"You're a funny little fuck. Okay, just for that, you're goin' down, bitch!"

"If that's what you think..."

"Did I stutter?"

"Blah, blah, blah."

Wayne grabbed a handful of darts and walked over to us. "Guess I'm gonna have to put you ladies to shame."

Doug and Joey laughed.

"Guess I'll have to teach you two," Wayne told them.

Doug gave my brother a strange look. "You'd be better off getting your tampons and joining the girls at the pool table."

"Oh, shit!" Joey roared. "He told you. Awe, the shit's flyin' now, boys!"

"I'm not worried about you guys," my brother continued.

"Shit, you better be," Quinn said. "You guys should all be shakin' in your shoes when this sucker starts after ya, you better run. The punishment is not good for anyone. May as well hand over your money now."

"Fat chance of that," Wayne replied.

Doug said, "Some good ol' shit-takin'. I fuckin' love it!"

"Can't say I didn't warn you," Quinn added.

"Not sure if you guys have heard this," Joey said, "but darts can predict the future."

Doug looked at him. "That right? I never heard any of that shit. Think you just made that up."

"I swear," Joey said in a calm voice.

"See it on the idiot box?"

"Read it."

"Oh, that makes it true? Oh, yes, crazy kids, believe everything you read. Our printed word would never lie to you. Come one, come all."

"You're too funny."

"And what did this article you read say about it?" Doug waved his beer in front of Joey's face.

"It was saying how when you throw a dart, wherever it goes dictates the outcome of your future. It said your mind unconsciously is at work. It was this long thing. It said your mind already knew what you would do."

"That's pretty deep."

"I don't believe any of it."

"Really?"

"Sounded like the person being interviewed was whacked-out on drugs or something."

"That happens. Makes you wonder, though."

"About what?"

"That you can just make something up. You can pull something out of your ass; no one's going to call you out on it at first."

"But, eventually..."

"Yeah. Guess you have a point."

"Word gets around."

"Ruin a man's rep."

"It was still interesting."

"I don't doubt it."

We spent a little while tossing the darts around. I held my own but lost. Joey won. He made a hundred bucks—not a bad sum. He made it a point to tell me and the other guys that we needed to practice the game.

We went back to the table and continued drinking. After talking and drinking, the girls approached us and wanted to dance. We went over to the dance floor.

We danced to a handful of songs.

Brandy and the girls said they were going to the

restroom. I always thought it funny when women went to the bathroom in packs. It was as if there was a green monster that would get them if they went in alone. It's just one of those things that kept my mind busy. I mean, you never saw guys doing that.

We continued talking. From a distance, I saw Donalyn laughing with one of the girls she came with. They went up to the bar and got some drinks. As I continued to look at Donalyn, I guess she sensed someone was looking at her; she looked around and then caught my eye. We smiled at each other. She gave a little wave. I waved back. She looked so fucking beautiful. I thought it'd be nice to walk up to her, kiss her, and give her a jump. I think she'd like it. I didn't know how a girl like that had no guy.

Awhile later, Brandy walked over to me.

"Hey," I said.

She took a drink of beer. "Oh, you missed me, babe? Thanks."

"Glad I can do my part. I wondered if you got lost, if you fell in the toilet or something."

"Not this time," she laughed.

"That's good."

"You can never be too sure."

"That's what I'm here for. I'm at your dis-posal."

She said, "What would I ever do without you?" she kissed me on the cheek. "You wouldn't know what to do. You'd probably become a loser or something."

She hit me on the arm. "Really? Okay, now, smart guy."

I shrugged. "Not everyone can be like me."

"Oh, don't I know it?"

I took her hand. "Having a good time?"

"Yeah."

"I'm glad," I told her. "There's more to come."

"Don't say?"

"When we get home."

"You think, huh?"

I looked at her. "Something tells me that's not gonna happen?"

She held her index finger in the air. "Ding!"

"Oh, I see how that goes. Okay. Why not, if I can ask?"

"Maybe," she sighed. "We'll have to see how things go."

"Still doesn't sound good to me."

"Never know," a grin rolled across her face.

"At least there's hope for me."

"Nice confidence."

"You have to be."

"Can't argue with that—it's important in a relationship. A lot of people lose that skill when they get into a relationship. Guess they figure they'll always keep the person they're with."

"Interesting way to look at it."

"But you don't have to worry. We'll be together forever."

"That's a long time."

She said, "When it's right, it's right."

I sat back and had a beer. "Seems like a good

night. Joey seems to be enjoying himself," I glanced over at Joey. He was laughing it up with the others. "I think he appreciates our support for the new gig."

"I'm sure he does," she said into her beer.

"You know, seeing him, it makes me think of my stuff."

"Whaddya mean?"

"Just the whole writing thing. I have the material; I need to get it into the right hands."

She got a little concerned look on her face. "Well, babe, I'm sure you'll be able to find someone."

"Hope so."

"Maybe your movie connections can help?"

"Different beast."

"New doors can open with them."

"Honestly, I don't wanna have anything to do with those people anymore. I got pushed out by the industry. Fuck them. I don't know; this whole thing annoys me. The future, wish I could see into it, you know?"

"I know, babe. It'll work itself out. Just have to keep doing what you've been doing."

"I know."

"I have faith in you."

"Think mine might be running out." "You shouldn't say that."

"If it's true, you can't escape it."

"You're bummed about the industry thing, it'll get better. Trust me. I liked all your stuff."

"You did?"

"I just didn't like that we were apart. I just wanted you to stay here. In a way, everything worked out."

"I just had to get my dreams ruined for that to happen."

She glared at me. "Oh, don't blame me. You could've still lived here and flew back-and-forth. Don't put that bullshit on me."

"I never said it was your fault."

She snapped. "Listen, asshole, I don't wanna get into a fight. We're here for a good time. We can talk about this later. We don't air dirty laundry in public."

"Fine with me," I said. "You started this whole thing. I was saying my feelings about the issue, that's all."

"This isn't the time or place."

"Agreed."

"Can we just drop it?"

"Sure."

"Good."

She said, "There's another day for that."

"I like the idea of writing novels. I think that may work. If I can find someone to publish, that'd be excellent."

She tapped her finger on the table. "I know what I know; I need more to drink."

She told me she would get some more drinks at the bar. I asked her to get me two more. Heather followed her path to the bar. Everyone was getting thirsty. A crowd was waiting for their orders. It took awhile for it to be her turn.

She came back with four beers and sat.

"Hey, Heather asked me if I wanna return to her house with the other girls."

"Whaddya guys gonna do?"

"Not sure. Maybe watch a movie, drink some wine, something like that. It's just too much here tonight. You can stay if you want. Guys need to enjoy yourselves."

"You sure?"

"Yeah. We'll be fine. You guys stay and have fun. I can get a ride with Heather."

"That's fine with me."

"You sure?"

"Yeah."

"Thanks, babe," she kissed me.

"You need any money?"

She shook her head. "No. I'm good."

We talked more as we drank.

She ran off to get her friends. A little while later, she came back with the girls. We chatted for a bit before they left.

14

As the night progressed, the boys and I shot a few pool games. I wasn't that great, but neither were they. None of us cared. We were never going to be pros or anything. We had fun drinking and laughing the night away. I wished Brandy would've stayed. I knew she was in good hands and nothing would happen to her. Even though they didn't say it, I'm sure the other guys wanted their girls to stay.

Joey started to tell us more about his new job. He told me I should get a job there. I loved music, but I couldn't see myself on the radio. Knowing me, I'd find somehow to fuck it up. After he talked to us a little about it, Doug started asking the most questions.

"If you'd like," Joey said, "you should come by the station with me some night. I'm sure it'll be fine."

"Might do that," Doug said. "We could do an interview and shit."

"What would we talk about?"

"I'm an interesting guy. Some of the things I've seen would make you shake in your shoes. Shit. I'm here to tell you. I'm the most fascinating person I know."

"I bet," I laughed.

Doug hit me. "Get fucked, bitch!"

I gave him a look. "You don't want any of this."

"Give it your best shot."

"You're a hoot, dude. I'd lay you out so hard. You wouldn't wake for about three weeks. You can put that in your fuckin' pipe and fuckin' smoke it, motherfucker."

We all laughed.

Joey looked at his beer, then at Doug. "We could just rap about movies or somethin'. Music is always a good topic. It's just the evolution of it all. You know, come to think of it, that'd be a good topic for my show. Make it a special few days. Every night would be a different style."

"You could do something like that?" Doug asked.

"Sure," Joey replied. "They said the night belongs to me. I'm free to do whatever. Just have to stay within the outline of the show."

Doug nodded. "I could get into something like that. Sounds like fun. Wish I had that freedom at my job."

"Really, what would you do with it? No offense, but it's just a factory."

"Hey," Doug wrinkled his face at him. "You sayin' you better than me?"

"No, no, no, I never said that. Do you want a job with me? Come down, talk to my boss, see what he says."

"Not sure I'd wanna do that."

"Why?"

"I like my hours."

I went to the restroom.

15

I did my business and came back out.

As soon as I walked out, I saw Donalyn walking toward me. The restroom for girls was beside the one for the boys.

As she got closer, I nodded. "How's it going?"

She stumbled a little as she walked.

"Pretty good, I guess," she smiled, making her forefinger and thumb like she would measure something tiny. "May have had a little too much to drink. I might've overdone it. I dunno... can't even think about that shit."

"I've heard that happens."

She said. "But...," she looked back at me, "I can still do this..." She did a little dance, shook her hips, twirled in a circle two times, and then did some footwork. "Yes, sir, I still got it. I can dance with the best of them," she stumbled a little. "I can go... I can go... I can... something.. those damn cows, that one thing...?"

"Until the cows come home?" I offered.

"Yeah," she pointed a finger at me. "That's the one."

"Well, that might get you outta a ticket later." She smiled. "Oh, man. Well, that's not going to happen. I'm not driving," she pointed over where the tables were. "We were just gonna take a cab."

"What about your car?"

"Just pick it up tomorrow."

"That's always good. That way, everyone can drink."

"That was the idea."

"It's not a bad one."

She had a big smile on her face. "I could use more."

"Think we all can."

A head shake. "Whaddya waitin' for? It's all about the night."

"What about you?"

She walked closer and looked me in the eyes. "Guess we'd better get more."

"Think that'd be the wise move," I nodded toward the women's restroom. "Were you needing to go in there?"

She shook her head. "No."

"Oh, okay, I just thought since you came over here..."

"No," she said. "I saw you were over here, thought I'd come over. Wanted to talk."

"About what?"

"I was thinking about you," she said. "Where'd your girlfriend go?"

"She went with Heather. Think this place got too loud for them."

"Too bad."

"How's that?"

"She left you here alone."

"Oh, it's okay. I don't mind. She wanted to spend time with her friends; I'm fine with that. She has her fun; I have mine."

"You didn't wanna go with her?"

"I wanted to stay here. The other guys didn't want to leave. I tried talking her into it."

"I see," she turned her head in the direction where the tables were, then back to me. "My friends, they don't wanna leave."

"We could join parties."

"We could."

"The guys would like that," I told her.

"I'm sure they would."

"Are they single?"

"They are."

"That'll be a plus in their book."

She started to sway back and forth a little. "Oh, you guys are all the same. Never a dull moment with you."

"We're a mystery. You can try to pry your way in."

"You won't open for me?"

I leaned against the bathroom door. "For you, anything."

"Thanks for that."

"Well, what about you?"

"What?" she swayed a little, brushing her hair from her face.

"You don't have a guy."

"How perceptive."

"It's all about the details," I chuckled. "Why don't you have a boyfriend?"

"Why?" Wanna be mine, man?"

" was thinkin' it a shame any guy would pass you by."

"I dunno. I just needed a break when I got here

after Texas.”

"Yeah. I'd heard about some of that. Well, that was a bad split. Heather was telling us about it."

"Oh."

"Which, by the way, you need to do that again."

"You think so?"

"Most differently."

"That's sweet of you to say. I'm going back soon. I'm not sure when. I got a lot of stuff. Tons of notebooks of things."

"We should combine talents."

"That's an idea. Yeah, I've seen the movies. I'm a fan. When's the next one getting here?"

I blinked a few times. "It's nice to have fans. No, I'm done with all of that."

"Why?"

"The politics of it all."

"Sorry to hear."

"It happens."

She got closer to me and draped her arms around my neck. The heat from her body was inviting.

"I'd like that," she said.

She moved in closer.

We kissed.

At first, I couldn't believe what I'd just done. I had always been a one-woman man. I had never cheated on anyone in my life. As I stared at her beautiful face, I ran through the ramifications of what would happen and how things would change forever. I'd never see her the same way. On the edge of my mind, Brandy was standing, calling out my name. I knew she'd get mad at me.

We kissed again.

I couldn't speak for her, but I was a fan.

As we kissed hard, I put my hands on her hips. She gave a light moan.

"Is this right?" I asked her.

"How's it feel?"

"Is it bad that I want more?"

"Not at all."

"Good," I took a gulp of air. "I want more."

She took her hand and ran it down the front of my shirt. "No one has to know. It can be our little secret," she looked into my eyes. "We can always go back to your place, get naked in bed, and read some poetry."

"A tempting offer... I'm with Brandy. We have a good thing going, you know?"

"I know," she sighed.

"Sorry."

"Just wish it wasn't... I met you too late, I guess."

"By a few years."

"I see."

"Don't feel bad."

"Doesn't help."

"Oh, I'm sure you'll be fine."

"Can't promise anything."

"This thing you're feeling, it'll pass."

"Heather said you and Brandy were having problems."

"She told you that?"

"Said it'd been going on for awhile."

"That's a private matter."

"Is it? Well, someone has to be there for comfort. It would help if you had someone to lick your wounds," she licked her lips and snickered.

"You could be right."

She placed her hand flat against my chest. "Hmmm, that's nice."

The heat of her slithered through me like a chunk of sunshine. She slid her hand slowly on my crotch. "We could go right here. Just go on the other side of the door."

"Might get in trouble for that. Could get kicked out."

A smile. "It'd be fun."

"Don't doubt that."

She dug her fingers to find the zipper to my pants.

She got the zipper halfway down before I put my hand on her hand to stop the unveiling. "Whaddya we waitin' for?" she asked.

"We shouldn't be here."

"Why?"

"You got bail money?" I asked.

"Nope. How much would we need?"

"Not sure. I've never had sex in the bathroom before. They could charge anything for that."

"There's a first for everything. I mean, come on, what's the worst that could happen? Jail?"

I laughed. "Sure, you wanna do it in the bathroom?"

"Why not?"

"It's just nasty."

She gave a nod.

Donalyn and I walked over to the table. I told the guys that she had been drinking a lot and wanted to go home and that I was going to take her.

She went over to where her friends were sitting and told them they should join my friends. They got up and went over to the table. We told them to all have a good time and not get too wild, or they'd get kicked.

We walked out of the bar into the cool air.

"A nice night," she said.

"It is," I looked up into the dark sky. "I wonder how many people are doing this now."

"Doing what?"

"Walking out of bars."

"Hopefully, a lot."

"Just makes you think."

We walked to where our cars were parked. We decided to take my car. I would take her back later for hers. Before we went to her place, we stopped by the store for more booze. We spent the next few hours drinking and having sweaty sex.

16

When I had time, I went to Wayne's and told him what happened. Earlier that day, Brandy and I got into a huge fight. It was the first time she'd talked about ending our relationship. Brandy had always been a little bipolar. I tried to support her best, but sometimes that wasn't enough. Over the years, she had terrible periods of depression. She attempted suicide a few times. I'm sure it was lonely for her when I was in California. She was all alone in Bencroft: In retrospect, that wasn't the best thing. If I could do it all over, I would've insisted she move with me or not go. In a lot of ways, I blamed myself. Getting mixed up with Donalyn didn't help matters at all.

"How's it going?" I asked.

"What's new with it?" Wayne said.

"About the same shit."

We went into the house. He got a few beers from the fridge.

"Where's Heather?" I asked him.

"She went over to Conway. I told her I didn't feel like going."

"I see."

"She's visiting a friend of hers."

"She looks anything like Donalyn?"

He laughed. "No, no, no, nothing like that. You know Lisa Morin?"

I thought for a minute. "Don't think so."

"She used to work at Hop n' Stop—blonde hair.

Nice body. Small tits."

I shrugged. "I dunno. I don't think so. I used to go in there. Guess I missed her."

"You probably saw her."

"Maybe."

"Well, anyway, that's where she went."

"And what are you left to do?"

"Not shit. Heather gave me a list, but I won't do it. She's not my boss. Fuck that shit," he took a drink. "Everything going good in Ethan's world."

"Brandy and I got into a fight," I told him. "Figured I'd come over here. Lay low for a bit until things cool down."

"When's that gonna be?"

"Not sure," I said. "Maybe all week."

He laughed.

"Nice to see my pain gives you joy."

He looked at me. "Have to lighten the situation. Sorry about that. What happened?"

"Her stupid shit," I shrugged. "We fought. It's all about the money."

"It always is."

I took a drink. "No kidding."

"She'll come around, right?"

"She always does. She gets in her moods. Give it a day or so; it'll be fine."

"You sure?"

"Yeah."

"That's good."

"It's just one of those thing. I dunno, I look at her sometimes, and I wonder."

"Wonder about what?"

"If she's the one."

My brother gave me a stern look. "That's some deep shit, dude."

"I know."

"Change can be what's needed sometimes.

"I can't do that to her. It's just a fight; we all have them."

"Heather and I have more than our share."

We moved into the living room. He sat on the couch; I took the armchair across from him. I looked around the room, trying to find the words for what I would tell my brother next.

I said, "The other night at the bar, when I took Donalyn home, we ended up having sex."

Wayne raised a brow. "That's interesting."

I shook my head. "I guess."

"That's some crazy shit, bro."

"I know, I know."

"Was it worth it?"

"It was."

"You gonna continue seeing her?"

"I think so, yes."

He sighed, said nothing for a minute, and opened his mouth. "Something like that, it just sounds..."

"What? Wrong?"

"I was gonna say that might be a fortunate thing."

"What do you mean?" I looked at him.

"If Brandy ever hits the road, you got her."

"Don't know if things are gonna go that way

yet."

"Well..."

"Hey, that's what I said. I'm not going to get too ahead of myself. Don't want things to back-fire." He gave me a little toast, and I laughed. I just shrugged and finished my beer. We went outside for a smoke. "You ever think of sneaking behind Heather?" I asked as I cracked open another beer

"I do," he rubbed his head. "I mean, I hadn't ever cheated on her. I've thought about it a few times. Sure. Everyone wants what they can't have; anyone will tell you that."

"Why'd you never do it?"

"Guess I never really got up the nerve. I could've easily done it, sure. After thinking about it, I couldn't bring myself to follow through. If I got caught, we'd get a divorce, simple as that."

I thought about that for a minute. "What if she never found out? What about then?"

"Maybe."

"See," I held my finger up.

"But I never did."

"They say a form of cheating is just thinking about it."

"Then we're all fucked."

"We just might."

"Still, I never acted on it."

"And I'm supposed to believe that?"

"You know me."

"I do. And I know you're all about the ladies.

Come on, you and Heather have only been together five years."

My brother laughed. "Yeah, if I wanna be with
her for more, I better not fuck it up. I hate to tell
you; they always find out somehow. No matter
how smart you think you are."

I took a drag off my cigarette and looked out
onto the road while a few cars passed. "Maybe
I'll be the loser after all this is over."

"What?"

I turned back to my brother. "Yeah, no matter
how this goes, someone will get hurt. When
Brandy finds out, it will be a huge shit-storm."

"But tell me," Wayne said, "why'd you go after
Donalyn?"

"I liked her from the start. That night at Funhouse, after that, I couldn't stop thinking about
her. I wanted to know more. It was fun and ex-
citing. I dunno, I found something in her that
Brandy didn't have."

"You thinking long-term with her? Break it off
with Brandy?"

"Not sure. I know when she finds out, it's going
to kill her."

"I can understand that."

"But still, that whole thing about being happy
with yourself. You have to do what's best for
you." Wayne threw his cigarette stub in the
bucket beside the door. "That changes all the
time."

"True."

He pointed at himself. "Don't get me wrong, I

like Brandy. She's a good girl. I'd hate to see you stay with someone you don't wanna be with."

"Know what you mean. I don't know. I wish I had one of those crystal balls.

"A gypsy, those are the only people they say can do that."

"Don't know any of those."

"Guess you're screwed."

"Maybe."

We talked for awhile over another smoke.

Over the next few weeks, Donalyn and I snuck around, enjoying each other when we could. As Donalyn and I spent time getting to know each other, I realized my feelings for Brandy were changing. Donalyn did a few more shows at Funhouse a few more times every time I was there. Since Donalyn and I knew many of the same people, keeping our secret was sometimes a little tricky. My friends, I'd use them as cover whenever I could. If I met Donalyn somewhere, I'd tell Brandy I was going to a friend's house. She was never the wiser.

We'd go to whatever place had the best drink specials every night. We had our favorites, but we were always looking for new ones. It was a great time to be alive. The circle I ran with had acquired a list of waiters and waitresses they enjoyed spending the night with.

17

One day, Brandy told me she would be working a double shift at work. As soon as she left, I called Donalyn, and she told me to come over. She moved into a new apartment. After I got a pack of cigarettes from a filling station, I headed to the apartment. I came to the building: It was a twenty-story wooden box. She lived on the nineteenth floor. I entered the lobby. A short, balding man called from behind the desk as I walked through the lobby to the elevator. The guy told me I had to sign in. I shuffled to the desk and signed a fake name into the book. I explained to the man I didn't know of such a rule and that he didn't need to be rude when he said something. It didn't help. He refused to make eye contact with me.

"Yes, yes, yes, sir," he said. "Sorry about that. It's the way it goes, you know?"

"Whatever."

"Hey, man, this is my arena, not yours." "Trust me, I don't want it."

"Thought so."

"Have fun with it, buddy."

"I'm here to serve."

I took the elevator to her floor. Walking down the tan and brown hallway, I noticed new occupants moving into the apartment beside Donalyn's. Two men carried a piano through the door while others came in with boxes. After negotiating my way through the madness, I knocked on her door. She answered. My mistress was dressed in a dark green cotton bathrobe. She leaned against the frame of the door and pointed her finger at me. "Hello, sir," she said. "I was hoping you'd call."

"As soon as I got a chance..."

She pulled me into the apartment. "I'm glad," she said, shutting the door behind me. I was getting a little lonely without you."

"I can change that."

"You better."

"I'll try my best."

"You do that."

I put my hands around her waist. I ripped open the belt, and the robe fell to the floor. We made our way to the white couch and fell. She dug her skinny fingers into my back while her hair spilled around her. I ran my hand under her panties and tore them off. I was looking at her naked body. The next thing I knew, my clothes were off, and we were indulging in one another. She ran her hand across my manhood. We were like wild cats, going at each other, bursting our passion, filling sexual desire. She took my dog in her hand and yanked a few times.

About an hour later, she was lying on top of me. Both of us were motionless. Her sweaty, naked body felt cool against my skin. "You're good," she whispered.

"I know."

"Just what I needed,' she picked herself up. "I

need to call you every day. Oh, man, that's what we must do every day."

"I'll be waiting."

"I bet. It's like... damn... when two puzzle pieces fit perfectly together, that's what it is."

"You better believe it, baby."

She put my hand in hers. "My knight in all the armor of the land, what would I do without you?"

"Good question. Take up golf?"

"Ha," she poked me in the chest with her finger. "Fat chance of that happening."

I laughed. "I like to play every once in awhile. It's not bad."

"I'll say, if you want a workout, that's a plan. Myself, I'd rather run on even ground."

I gave a nod. "Sure, I can see that. Don't wanna go twisting those ankles or anything."

"Exactly."

"Gotta do what you gotta."

She brushed a few hairs from her face. "Want something to drink?"

"Sure."

She stood from the couch and walked across the carpet into the kitchen, looking in the fridge. "I have soda, beer, and Iced Tea."

"Sweet or un-sweet?"

"Sweet," she took the jug out of the fridge. "I made it the other day."

"Tea's always refreshing."

"Also, have some whiskey and wine in the cabinet."

"Tea's fine."

"Okay. You got it."

"I'm not ready to start drinking right now," I said. "I might have some later. We can smoke some dope, too. I have some with me."

"Sure, we can do that a little later. I'm a firm believer in that everything's better with pot."

I lit a cigarette from my pack.

She was a good lover. We spent the rest of the day talking and getting high.

18

I woke up one morning to Brandy standing over me. She told me that she knew all about me cheating on her. She told me that if I wanted that, she couldn't live there anymore. She moved out and got with a singer of a band.

Donalyn and I moved in together.

www.ingramcontent.com/pod-product-compliance
Lightning Source LLC
Chambersburg PA
CBHW061127100726
47911CB00013B/712